I'm Brown
and My Sister Isn't

Written by Robbie O'Shea
Illustrated by Matthew Ambre

Robbie O'Shea

RKO Enterprises, 2002

Copyright of the text: Robbie O'Shea, 2002
Copyright of the illustrations: Matthew Ambre, 2002
Book layout and design by Maria Ambre

Editorial, sales and distribution, rights and permission inquiries should be addressed to RKO Enterprises, PO Box 117, LaGrange, IL 60525-0117

Manufactured in the United States of America

THE LIBRARY OF CONGRESS HAS CATALOGED THIS EDITION
AS FOLLOWS:
First Edition
I'm Brown and My Sister Isn't
by Robbie O'Shea
2002100655

ISBN:0-9718034-0-4

This work is dedicated
to all of the brave children in the world,
especially Amanda & Christopher
and Ari & Lauren.

nd, in fond memory of Ms. Robbie Johnson,
a mentor like no other.

A special heartfelt thank you
to all the angels
that made this work possible.

Author's note: This book discusses differences from the child of
color's point of view. It was my intent to give the child of color a
positive and active voice in the racial discussion.

I'm brown and my sister isn't.

I'm a boy and my sister isn't.

We're both adopted.

I like trucks and trains,
my sister doesn't.

My sister likes dolls
and frilly things,
I don't.

We both like vacations.
I get a tan,
my sister gets a sunburn.

We both go to school.
We both have lots of friends.

Our family is special
for many reasons,

but mostly because
I'm brown and my sister isn't!

About the author: Robbie O'Shea, PhD is the adoptive mother of two children. She enjoys teaching full-time in the Physical Therapy Program at Governor's State University, Illinois. Her clinical area is pediatrics and neurology. She is actively involved with the local adoption community and is Vice President of Chicago Area Families for Adoption. She lives with her children and husband near Chicago, IL. This is her first book.

About the illustrator: Matthew Ambre's work as an illustrator is well-known and diverse. He has illustrated for advertising and more recently has worked in the fine arts arena. His latest children's book is "The Rescue of Baby Jessica", a second grade reader for McGraw-Hill. Mr. Ambre grew up in Iowa and studied Illustration and Design at Columbus College of Art and Design in Columbus, OH. He now resides in Chicago with his artist wife, Maria.